Dear Parent:
Your child's love of reading starts here!

Every child learns to read in a different way and at his or her own speed. Some go back and forth between reading levels and read favorite books again and again. Others read through each level in order. You can help your young reader improve and become more confident by encouraging his or her own interests and abilities. From books your child reads with you to the first books he or she reads alone, there are I Can Read Books for every stage of reading:

SHARED READING
Basic language, word repetition, and whimsical illustrations, ideal for sharing with your emergent reader

BEGINNING READING
Short sentences, familiar words, and simple concepts for children eager to read on their own

READING WITH HELP
Engaging stories, longer sentences, and language play for developing readers

READING ALONE
Complex plots, challenging vocabulary, and high-interest topics for the independent reader

ADVANCED READING
Short paragraphs, chapters, and exciting themes for the perfect bridge to chapter books

I Can Read Books have introduced children to the joy of reading since 1957. Featuring award-winning authors and illustrators and a fabulous cast of beloved characters, I Can Read Books set the standard for beginning readers.

A lifetime of discovery begins with the magical words **"I Can Read!"**

Visit www.icanread.com for information
on enriching your child's reading experience.

For Crismary Lopez, the smartest
third grader I know!
—J.O'C.

For Janet Bass—one of the many
great librarans I've met along the road
—R.P.G.

For busker-wizard JS, who when I was a NYC
newbie showed me that bubble magic was
indeed a wondrous thing
—T.E.

I Can Read Book® is a trademark of HarperCollins Publishers.

Fancy Nancy: Bubbles, Bubbles, and More Bubbles!
Text copyright © 2018 by Jane O'Connor
Illustrations copyright © 2018 by Robin Preiss Glasser
All rights reserved. Manufactured in China.
No part of this book may be used or reproduced in any manner whatsoever without written permission except in the case of
brief quotations embodied in critical articles and reviews. For information address HarperCollins Children's Books, a division of
HarperCollins Publishers, 195 Broadway, New York, NY 10007.
www.icanread.com

Library of Congress Control Number: 2017943437
ISBN 978-0-06-237790-6 (trade bdg.) — ISBN 978-0-06-237789-0 (pbk.)

17 18 19 20 21 SCP 10 9 8 7 6 5 4 3 2 1 ❖ First Edition

I Can Read!

BEGINNING 1 READING

Fancy NANCY

Bubbles, Bubbles, and More Bubbles!

by Jane O'Connor

cover illustration by Robin Preiss Glasser

interior illustrations by Ted Enik

HARPER

An Imprint of HarperCollinsPublishers

Ooh la la!

I have splendid news!

(Splendid is fancy for great.)

Tomorrow our class

is seeing *The Big Bubble Show.*

Ms. Glass has been teaching us about bubbles.

"Bubbles always come out round,"
I tell my family.

"I will prove it."

I blow into a square wand.

Voilà—round bubbles!

I blow into a star wand.

Voilà! More round bubbles.

Then I demonstrate—

that means show—

how to hold a bubble.

(Dunk your hand

in bubble mix first.)

Later the bell

outside my room rings.

Oh no!

There is horrendous news.

(Horrendous means very, very bad.)

Bree is sick.

She cannot go

to *The Big Bubble Show.*

I am very sad.

It won't be as much fun

without Bree there.

The next day

all through the show

I think of Bree.

I wish she could see

the bubble snowfall

and the bubbles

filled with smoke

and a hat made of bubbles

that lands on Lionel's head.

The finale is the best part.

(Finale is fancy for the end.)

It is a bubble ballet.

The dancers make giant bubbles
that float to the music.
It is magical to watch!

At home,

There is a message from Bree.

More horrendous news!

She will not be back

at school before Friday.

"Was the bubble show great?"

she writes.

I do not want to make her feel bad.

So all I write back is

"It was pretty good."

That night

I perform—that means act—

for my family.

I dance like the dancers

in the finale.

Then suddenly

a bubble goes *POP!*

inside my head.

I have an idea.

Ms. Glass and the kids

think it is a splendid idea.

We make up a bubble dance.

We leap and spin and twirl

all over the place.

On Friday

Bree is back.

The front of the room

is our stage.

There is a sign.

It says, "A Bubble Ballet for Bree."

Bree sits up front.

She is the audience.

(An audience means the people

watching a show.)

Ms. Glass puts on the music
and—*voilà!*—
we start dancing.

It is not easy dancing

and blowing bubbles

at the same time.

(Try it and you'll see.)

26

Are we as good as the dancers

at the show?

No.

Are our bubbles as big?

No.

Does Bree enjoy our ballet anyway?

Yes! Yes! Yes!

At the end we bow and curtsy.

Bree stands and claps.

"Bravo!" she whispers.

(She can't shout.

Her throat still hurts a little.)

Bree asks us to do

the bubble dance again.

This time she joins in.

And guess what?

She blows the biggest bubble of all.

Fancy Nancy's Fancy Words

These are the fancy words in this book:

Audience—people watching a show

Demonstrate—show

Finale—the end

Horrendous—very bad

Perform—act

Splendid—great